Strange Tales 2

Darren Joaquim Silva

ISBN: 978-0-9576401-9-1
ISBN 13

~ The world wants to be deceived, so let it be deceived ~

CONTENTS

Don't Dance With Tomorrow

Suzel wasn't the same after the miscarriage. It had been over a month, but it still felt like shards of glass were in her stomach, cutting her from the inside. As she rested her head on the cold rattling window, the bus jolted and her handbag fell. She blushed as her pregnancy test rolled along the floor. She immediately grasped it before anyone noticed. A lump formed in her throat when she read the display again.

"Not Pregnant."

A hot flush crawled inside her abdomen. She swiftly opened the window, and the smell of November rain permeated the bus. A mother sitting near the front, bounced her baby on her knee to hush its crying. Suzel flashed her a faint smile before her exhausted sigh fogged the window. Suddenly the bus braked and its engine switched off.

"This bus will now terminate here," said the mechanical voice.

The lights dimmed and the doors opened. Moans from passengers filled the silence until they eventually clambered off. Streetlamps lit the dark cobbled path and rain pelted Suzel as she dashed through the park. She turned a corner and halted. The path ahead was barricaded as a funfair was being rigged. She grimaced as her heels pierced the mud as she crept around the blockade. In the foreground, a circus tent struggled to stay grounded and the shutters of a ghost house violently fluttered. Her suit was dripping wet and desperately needing shelter, she ran inside a purple tent next to a crooked tree.

The subtle clanging of a wind chime soothed her as she admired the numerous dream catchers and Mayan relics dispersed around. But nestled in the corner, covered in a black velvet cloth was a wooden box.

Suzel staggered over and removed the cover.

Inscribed on the wood was a Latin phrase.

"Cras Es Noster."

Suzel ran her nails over the groove and unlocked it.

The inside was padded with a crystalline ball rooted in its centre. She examined it in the fading light. The ball was eerily foreboding and a dormant insect was stuck inside it. Her nose twitched and she sneezed.

'Bless you,' said a voice behind her.

Suzel screamed and quickly retuned the box. In front of her was an old lady.

'I'm so sorry!' she panted. 'It was pissing down with rain and I needed shelter.'

The old lady twisted her head like a curious hound.

'Take a seat, my name is Neviah.'

'No, I can't… That's really nice of you, but I have to go. My husband must be worried sick.'

Suzel pulled her handbag over her shoulder. Raindrops pounded the grass, and beyond the oak trees lightning flashed the sky. Neviah, impervious to the booming thunder, simply poured some tea. Suzel relented and studied Neviah as she sat. Her face was shriveled and her eyes were unusually far apart. Her voice, although raspy, lingered like honey dripping off a spoon.

'I don't mean to be rude, but who are you?
A fortuneteller... a clairvoyant... a psychic?'

'Yes my dear, I can see so far into the future, that
I'm already over my next husband.'

A smile emerged on her shriveled face.

'Old fortune teller joke,' she added.

Suzel smiled and let the steam from the mug
comfort her. Neviah's eyes narrowed - like she was
glaring into a crack in Suzel's soul.

'There is quiet determination in your eyes...'

Suzel's blushed and glanced away.

'That's fine my dear, I'm not a therapist. But, you
did seem fascinated with something else?'

Suzel sheepishly looked up.

'That box - veiled from human eyes for dutiful
reason. You were looking at it when I came in?'

'I was just curious.'

'And what happened when you looked inside?'

'Nothing, it was just a crystal ball.'

Neviah strummed her fingers over her relics. 'Of all my
possessions, you chose this... or maybe it chose you?'

She dropped the box on the table.

Dust flew and the silver clasp unlocked itself.

'*Cras Es Noster*' - What does it mean?' asked Suzel.

'It's Latin for 'Tomorrow Is Ours.''

Neviah delicately handled the crystal ball.

'This artifact is centuries old. They say it has the power to control fate… However it comes with a deadly price. A mere reading will steal years from your life as a trade off. And since you are not aware of the day you perish, it makes it a dance. So I ask you Suzel… do you dare dance with tomorrow?'

'What do you mean?'

'Would you like a reading?'

Suzel scrunched her face in disbelief.

'To be honest, nothing seems to be going my way. I feel like I'm in some sort of purgatory.'

'Time is the only purgatory my dear.'

Suzel peered into her handbag. Numerous bills and the negative pregnancy test glared back at her. She tucked her hair behind her ear and looked up.

'So it's basically just a reading?'

'No. This will accurately foretell a sector, which will benefit you.'

Suzel shrugged her shoulders. 'Okay… sure.'

Neviah smirked and held out the ball. She closed her eyes and a humming sound protruded from her cracked lips. Suzel rolled her eyes. But just before she grabbed her handbag, the ball suddenly flashed. Suzel leaned forward in awe. Neviah's humming intensified and the creature inside the ball moved. Suzel jumped back. It was a hybrid of scorpion and spider, and its sharp pincers clinked as it crawled around the inside of the glass. Neviah's eyes opened. They were now dilated and bloodshot.

"**For the fame you seek. A colour of red will ascend your peak**…"

The creature halted and the ball ceased flashing. Neviah quickly placed it back in the box. She wheezed as she covered it with the cloth. Suzel anxiously stood.

'So that's all you have for me? A silly rhyme?'

'Do not mock the hand of fate.'

'Great… so how much do I owe you?'

'Nothing dear. You have already paid.'

The rain had calmed and Suzel headed outside.

'Anyway I should get going, thanks… for the tea.'

When Suzel got home, her husband Mark was asleep

on the couch. A meager light from the TV lit the room. A reporter was interviewing Douglass Fulton, an unpleasant candidate for the upcoming general election. Suzel switched it off before he could spout his rhetoric. She removed her heels and her damp feet slid on the hardwood floor as she crept upstairs.

When she returned from the shower, Mark was waiting for her in the bedroom.

'Well… how'd it go?'

'They want a redraft of my election article.'

'Not about work… the test.'

'I don't want to talk about it. You won't believe the day I've had,' said Suzel as she climbed into bed.

'So it was negative… again?'

'Everything seems negative at the moment.'

'Get some sleep. Things will get better in time…'

Suzel buried herself under the blanket as the shower hissed around the room.

'The strangest thing happened to me today…'

'Hold that thought!' yelled Mark from the shower. 'So I was talking to my boss earlier, she mentioned something about lunar conception.'

Suzel bit her tongue in frustration.

'I know, I know, it sounds like pseudoscience but its linked to the moon and melatonin. Maybe it could work? Research it when you have time.'

The hiss of the shower ceased and Mark poked his head out. 'Anyway, what were you saying?'

'Never mind.'

The next morning, the sky was a cloudless blue and the streets were filled with puddles from yesterdays storm. Suzel hopped off the tube and crossed the busy road, but out of nowhere; a bus sped into a pothole and drenched her with murky rainwater. Suzel screamed. Onlookers and tourists looked on and laughed. She chased the bus to reprimand the driver, but it was now just a red speck in the distance.

Suzel wrung her pencil skirt in the toilet of a nearby coffee shop. She ordered a coffee and waited by the window. A covert meeting with two men was taking place in the alleyway. Her jaw dropped as she slowly gleaned one of them was Douglas Fulton. She hid behind a newspaper and hit record on her phone. A confrontation broke out and one of the men handed Douglass a small sachet. They soon dispersed and Suzel stopped recording. She dashed to her office and immediately called her senior editor.

'Suzel has anyone else seen this?' he questioned.

'No, it just happened now!'

'This will hit the front page Suzel! I can see it now… "Douglass bites the dust!"

'Or how about "Douglas suffers a huge blow?"' Mark awoke to the sound of Suzel furiously typing. The laptop light forced his tired eyes to squint.

'Suzel its almost 3AM. Get some sleep.' She ignored him and continued to hammer at the keyboard. He sighed and covered his ears with the pillow. By morning, the story had reached the four corners of the globe. When Suzel finally arrived home, Mark was waiting for her with a newspaper in hand.

'I couldn't believe my eyes when I saw your name next to the article!' he remarked. He handed her the paper and she flicked through it with a smile. However as she scanned the page, she bit her tongue in angst. Next to her column was an advertisement for the local funfair. Suzel jittered and dropped the paper.

'What's the matter?' he asked.

'Nothing,' she mumbled. 'Just a coincidence.'

◆

Suzel's stared longingly at the frothy heart dissolving in the centre of her latte. Her eyes were bloodshot from working overtime, a consequence of her famous article. A vendor nudged the table and spilled her coffee as he distributed a leaflet.

"FUN FAIR – FREE ENTRY - ONE WEEK LEFT"

The neon lights from the carousel threw vivid colours onto everyone's winter coats. Screams from children riding the helter-skelter made Suzel wince as she trudged through the crowd towards the tent.

'I thought I would see you again,' muttered Neviah. 'Sorry another fortune teller joke,' she added.

Suzel faked a smile.

'I need another reading… now.'

'You have more audacity than sense my dear.' Suzel sat across from her. 'My mother always used to say, "If the future scares you, do something about it, it's coming whether you like it or not."

'A wise woman,' muttered Neviah.

'Please, just one more time and that's it! I know it sounds strange, but the phrase came true… there was this red bus and I followed it and it…'

'Good fortune is a fickle God my dear.' Neviah closed the curtains and slowly withdrew the insidious crystal ball. She held it in her palm but at the last second veiled it with her long fingers. An expression of scorn flashed across Suzel's face.

'I hope you haven't forgotten the price of this reading?' asked Neviah. 'This could potentially steal crucial years from your life and if…'

'I'm aware,' rebuffed Suzel.

Neviah uncoiled her fingers and the crystal ball flashed. The creature awoke and this time, a small crack appeared on the ball. Suzel grasped the tablecloth as it wriggled around.

'… **For the wealth you wish. Seek rainfall to find your bliss**.'

The creature violently hissed and Suzel shrieked. Neviah's hands trembled as she flung the ball back in the box.

'These readings are a pyrrhic victory for you and me. This is the last time,' said Neviah as she ushered

Suzel to the door.

'But what if I don't get what I need?'

'And what is it you need my dear?'

Suzel's eyes darted to the pregnancy test in her handbag.

◆

"Happy Birthday! See you tonight at the restaurant. The tables booked for 7:30PM. Love Mark."

Suzel put her phone away and stared at a passenger's umbrella, which was dripping rainwater onto the train seat. Her breathing became erratic. The doors opened and she barged commuters from her path as she ran through the station in her heels. The wind lashed rain over her face as Neviah's message danced across her mind. 'Seek rainfall to find your bliss?'

When Suzel arrived at the restaurant, she was drenched and downtrodden. Mark clenched his teeth as she trudged over.

'Where the hell have you been? It's 8:30PM.'

'Sorry I got stuck in the office.'

She put her wet coat over the chair and sat down.

'You're soaking wet.'

Suzel seized the wine and poured herself a glass.

'What are you doing? We're trying for a baby.'

Mark looked at her like she was a complete stranger.

'Last week you finally got the break you wanted; yet you still seemed so upset. You haven't been eating, or sleeping. Can you just tell me what's wrong?'
Mark put his hands over Suzel's cold shaking fingers.

'You heard what the doctor said about alcohol and fertility,' he added.

'I don't need a doctor, I have something far more potent… fate.'

'Fate? What are you talking about?'

Suzel raised her glass. 'Cheers!' She downed the wine and exhaled. Mark slammed his fist on the table and the cutlery bounced.

'Don't give me that look Mark. I have a chance to make things better.'

'Make things better? For whom?'

'We can have anything we desire. I just need to solve this…'

Suzel abruptly stood and peered around the restaurant like a possessed woman.

'I need to get back in the rain.'

19

Before Mark could intervene, she ran towards the exit. The floor was still wet with speckled drops of rain and she slipped. Her head smashed off the edge of a table and she fell backwards onto the cold marble floor.

◆

Suzel felt something crawl between her toes and tossed the blanket aside. The creature from the crystal ball wriggled up her leg. Suzel pressed her palms into the mattress, but it's pincers dug into her skin as it crawled across her abdomen. It violently hissed and repeatedly stabbed her with its stinger. Suzel screamed and thrashed around the bed. She opened her eyes. Her skull throbbed with pain and she felt a bandage around her head.

'Mark! Where am I? What happened?'

'You're in the hospital. You had a bad accident.'

Suzel leered at an IV drip that was secreting a pink liquid into her body.

'They had to pump your blood. Apparently it was full of caffeine pills.'

Suzel shamefully pressed her head into the pillow.

'Well if it makes you feel any better, our lawyer said you'd get a big payout. And not having a wet floor sign won't help the restaurants defence either. Some late birthday present eh?'

'What do you mean late birthday present?'

'You've been out for two days. The nurse said its best if you stay one more…'

'No… No! Give me my handbag. Now!'
Suzel dug through her possessions like a feral cat. The soggy funfair flyer lay at the bottom of her purse.

'Today's the last day,' she whispered.

'The last day?'

'Nothing… erm. I really need to rest.'

Mark kissed her and headed to the door.

'Listen, I spoke to the nurse about our situation. She said managing stress levels is vital for conceiving. So please get some rest okay? I love you.'

Suzel flashed him a meek smile. Once he'd left she immediately removed the IV drip and got dressed. Whilst in search for the exit, Suzel stumbled upon the maternity ward. A sharp pain formed in her chest, as she gazed at the mothers tending to their newborns. She gasped as she barely recognized herself in the windows reflection. She unwrapped her bandage and quivered. Her skin was a bruised purple, and her eyes were dangerously dilated.

Evening twilight poured through the park and leaves fell from the trees, as hoards of builders dismantled the rides. Suzel slipped inside the tent. Most of Neviah's belongings were packed away. She clawed her way through the boxes and tossed her relics aside.

'Those who are ignorant of power, will soon be ruled by it,' said Neviah clutching the box.

'I need you to do a final reading!'

'And I need you to leave.'

Suzel sprung at her and tried to snatch the box.

'There's one more thing I need!' she begged. She pounced on her again, but this time Neviah moved aside and Suzel crashed out of breath. Neviah inspected the ghastly scar on her head.

'What happened to you my dear?'

Tears cascaded down Suzel's face as she struggled to rise to her feet.

'I don't want money or fame Neviah… I want a child! My husband and me, we've been trying for years.

It's all we bloody talk about! And since the miscarriage… I'm not myself, let alone have I shaken the phantom pitter-patter of unborn feet kicking the inside of my stomach. Do you have any idea how it feels? Especially when everyone pokes their noses in? "So when are you and Mark gonna have a little one?" "Am I going to be a grandmother soon?" or my personal favourite - "You never understand life until it grows inside of you." I'm just fearful that my time is running out! If this can help me, I have to do it.'

Neviah loosened her grip on the box.

'You are hanging onto this life by your fingernails,' she warned as she unlocked the box.

Suzel nervously placed her palms on the table.

'This is your last chance to leave,' added Neviah. Suzel remained in her seat. Neviah's fingers dug into Suzel's wrists, and numerous cracks appeared on the crystal ball as the creature thrashed around.

"Too long you have been immune. Look skyward for a crescent phase of fortune."

A huge fissure appeared on the ball. The creature locked eyes with Suzel and viciously snarled. Blood poured from Neviah's nose and dripped onto the table.

Petrified, she threw the ball back into the box.

This time, she locked it with a key.

'Please Neviah, help me decipher its meaning?'

Neviah pushed her outside.

'I wish you happiness for the years you have left…'

Neviah shut the curtain and zip locked the tent.

'Please Neviah, I have no idea what it means!'

Suzel screamed until her lungs went sore, but Neviah refused to answer. Suzel surrendered and sat on the swings in the empty playground. Teardrops stained her jeans as she tried to force her thoughts into an order of semblance, but Neviah's premonition pierced her like a bullet in the side. A cloud passed over the crescent moon, and hurled the playground into darkness. Suzel gazed skyward and waited patiently for the pale glow of the moon to reemerge.

◆

Fuzzy pink remnants of candyfloss melted in the sun. Mark helped Suzel off the carousel and handed back her red balloon. He held her small hand as they walked through the hoards of screaming teenagers.

A fell wind blew and Suzel's balloon left her grasp. She let go of Mark's hand and chased after it. He yelled for her to come back, but the music from the waltzers deafened his pleas. The balloon danced on the winds breath and became stuck in the branches of a crooked tree. Mark finally caught her. He crouched and hugged her tight. An old lady appeared and snagged the balloon from the branch.

'Sorry! My daughter loves to run off on her own.'

The old lady's lips curved into a smirk.

'Just like her mother I presume.'

Mark's face went pale.

'Yeah… But her mother sadly… how did you…'

The old lady returned the balloon and caressed Suzel's hair.

'Fate has brought you here my dears. Come inside for a free reading. For some the flow of time is gentle and for others it is cruel, but let it not be that way. We are prisoners of the present, stuck in a past we can no longer access, and a future we apparently cannot see…'

One Fine Day

Malcolm gazed into the rearview and watched the pine trees sway in the breeze. He accelerated around the winding mountain road and past a crooked sign that read "Drive Carefully." The car engine groaned like a harpooned whale and his wife Melody, grit her teeth.

'Is that the engine?' she asked.

'Strange, I checked it before we left.'

'I'll call my parents and tell them we might be late.'

'No… don't call. Everything will be fine.'

A fork appeared in the road and the GPS distorted.

'Shit!' yelled Malcolm as he shook the screen.

'Didn't you bring a map?' asked Melody.

'I think I left it at the candlestick makers… Of course I didn't bring a map! We have GPS now.'

'Had GPS Malcolm. Had! Well you can explain to my mother why we'll be late for thanksgiving dinner.'

Malcolm arbitrarily drove down one of the paths.

'Do you even know where you're going?'

'You worry too much… Everything will be fine.' Melody shuddered and kissed her crucifix pendant.

Their car deteriorated upon arrival at a rural gas station. There was a retro diner in the distance, and as they exited the car, the sun hid behind the clouds and a cold shadow fell over Melody's face.

'Where are we?' she asked.

Malcolm shrugged his shoulders. He withdrew his mobile but it had no signal. A skinny man wearing an oil blemished baseball cap emerged from the gas station. His neck was covered in scars and he bit some beef jerky as he approached them.

'I'm Eddie, the proprietor of this here gas station. What can I do for ya?'

'Our car broke down,' muttered Melody.

He inspected the fuel gauge and wiped his oily fingers over his dungarees.

'Why don't you folks rest in that diner? I'll have a look at the engine for you.'

Melody discreetly shook her head at Malcolm.

'Erm that's nice but, we really need to get going. We're heading to my in laws house you see,' he added.

Eddie glared right through him.

'I've met tree stumps in Louisiana with a higher IQ than you. This engines a mess, and you're all outta brake fluid.'

Malcolm bit his tongue and turned to Melody.

'We'd much prefer to just call for help,' she interrupted. She took out her phone and her face turned red. Eddie smirked.

'No signal eh? There's a payphone in that diner… My older brother Andy runs that place. Tell him I sent you.'

He put the wrench in his mouth and hummed a tune as he inspected the engine.

'We're not going inside Malcolm,' she whispered.

'Listen, everything will be fine. We'll just use the payphone and leave.'

A muddy tow truck was parked outside. A broken neon sign above glowed "**D I** N **E** R" however it only flashed the words "die." Melody gave him a stern look.

'They really should get that fixed,' he muttered.

Rock music echoed from inside as they pushed open the door. It was so loud they could no longer whisper. The floor was tiled and sticky, and the smell of bacon clung to the air. A man in a stained white vest was cooking behind the counter. Melody spotted the payphone and hurried over. She grabbed the receiver but quickly realized the wire had been cut. She slammed it down and scurried back to Malcolm.

'The phone doesn't work. We have to leave now!'

Malcolm leaned over the counter and turned the volume down on the radio.

'You must be Andy? We need you to call the cops.'

He turned around and scowled.

'What you folks need the cops for?'

'Car trouble,' said Malcolm.

His scowl evolved into a sly smirk.

'Well I can't help you. Our payphone hasn't worked since 98.'

Before returning to the stove, he peered through the kitchen blinds and noticed his brother with their car. 'I'm shutting up shop. Last orders.'

He cracked an egg on the stove and flipped it with a rusty tong.

'We haven't eaten in hours. We might as well order something,' whispered Malcolm.

Melody grimaced as the man coughed a green phlegm into the bin.

'I have tic-tac's in my purse,' she replied.

Malcolm grabbed a menu.

'Erm… I'll have a ham and cheese melt.'

'All I've got is eggs.'

'Okay, I'll have that on some sourdough toast.'

The man used the tong to scratch his back and started cooking. They sat in a booth by the window and tried to admire the purple sky.

Andy soon approached them and put a plate down. The egg was runny and had leaked over the side. He tossed two cloudy glasses down. The water spilled over the rim and onto the table. He limped back and disappeared through the kitchen door. Malcolm bit into the sandwich and regrettably chewed.

'How is it?' she asked.

'I can't wait for your mom's mac and cheese.'

He took a sip of water. 'And the water's warm…'

31

Melody pushed her glass aside and peered out the window. 'Malcolm! The car! Where's our car?!'

He leaned over and looked outside.

'Okay relax, he might have just moved it.'

'Moved it! Where?'

The diner door swung open. Eddie sheepishly walked over. He removed his cap and held it like he'd just witnessed a kitten drown to death.

'Well folks, I have some good news and bad news. Bad news is, your car can't be fixed till tomorrow morning. But the good news is, I've spoken to my brother and we'll give you a lift to the nearby lodge.'

Melody buried her face in her hands.

'We'll just stay here till sunrise,' she added.

'Nonsense! It's thanksgiving, can't have you folks wandering around like a fart in a fan factory.'

The tow-truck's headlights pierced the window. Malcolm realized their car was pitched onto the trucks hook. Eddie locked the diner and put his arm around Malcolm. His brother was in the drivers seat smoking a cigar.

'Don't be shy, plenty of room if we squeeze in tight,' he muttered.

Malcolm put one foot inside the truck.

'Malcolm no!' yelled Melody.

Eddie leered at her over his shoulder.

'Sorry, it's very kind of you, but we really need to get to my parents house,' she added.

'And how do you spose you're gonna get there?' Melody bit her nails to stop her hands from trembling.

'Quit your yapping and get in the truck will yah?'

'Andy!' Eddie scolded his brother in the car.

'Sorry bout him. Listen we'll take you folks to the lodge. Our ma runs it, so you can rest up for the night. I'll have your car fixed by sunrise - free of charge - how's that sound?'

Melody's intuition pounded her rib cage.

'Come on Mel, what other choice do we have?'

'Okay...'

It was dark and Melody had no idea where they were going. The narrow beam of the trucks headlights lit the gloomy road, until the car violently swerved and the road replaced itself with mud. Branches smacked the windshield and Melody shrieked.

'Where are we going!?'

'Shortcut,' muttered Andy.

'Malcolm? No! Stop the car!' she yelled.

'We shoulda left em on the side of the road!
I told you Eddie, they got wise blood,' muttered Andy.

'Don't mind him. We always take this shortcut.'

The truck pulled up on a muddy bank. Eddie
stepped out. Malcolm and Melody followed him
outside. He took out a knife and hacked at the willow
tree branches. A decrepit sign covered in bird shit read

"COZY MOTEL"

'I thought you said it was a lodge?' asked Melody.

'Well we're still rebranding. Hollywood's given
motels a bad rap… Lodge sounds more inviting.'

'Yeah so does the "Four Seasons," joked Malcolm.
Eddie didn't laugh. 'Well we have to park the car. Just
follow that path straight to the lodge. Ma should still
be awake. Make sure you tell her Eddie sent yah.'

Malcolm and Melody helplessly watched the car
speed off into the darkness.

'Now's our chance to run,' she whispered.

'Run? We're in the middle of nowhere!'

'You just had to get in the frigging car Malcolm!'

'Listen, we'll just head inside, call your parents, and
everything will be fine.'

Moonlight trickled through the branches and mosquitoes buzzed as they trudged through the nettles. The motel was a towering grey structure covered in moss. Beside the porch was a tree stump with a chainsaw stuck in it. Malcolm knocked on the door, but it was already open. The foyer was dim and a dusty carpet stretched towards the reception.

'Malcolm this is like something from a horror film, let's just leave!'

A light bulb flickered over the guest book and he pressed the service bell.

'See, no one's home. Let's go,' she added.

The reception door creaked open, but no one appeared. Melody screamed as two black cats leapt on the table.

'That's just Lulu and Lizzie. They don't scratch.' Melody caught her breath. A hunched woman edged around the desk. Her hair was patchy and she wore a cardigan over a purple nightgown.

'I wasn't expecting any guests,' she muttered.

'Hi… we had some car trouble, Eddie sent us.'

She suddenly halted and grinned. 'Did he now?'

She banged the guestbook with her walking stick.

'Sign here please… insurance purposes.'

Malcolm flicked through the pages. There were no other signatures.

'Does the room have a phone?'

'Unfortunately the crows severed the power lines.'

Melody jittered and cursed under her breath. Malcolm handed her some cash, but she pursed her lips and shook her head.

'If my boy sent you, your money is no good here.'

Malcolm pocketed his cash, and they followed her down the dim hall.

'My name's Jan and breakfast isn't included.' She stopped at door 237 and took out a bunch of keys. She opened the room and led them inside.

'Here it is… The honeymoon suite. Would you like a wake up call?'

'No thanks,' said Malcolm.

'Enjoy your stay,' she said and slammed the door. Melody immediately bolted it with the chain. Malcolm sat on the bed and flicked on the static TV.

'We have to let someone know we're here.'

'Well I hope you have a flare gun in your purse.'

'I'm serious Malcolm, they might murder us.'

'Relax… everything will be fine,' he said as he

yawned and closed his eyes.

'Malcolm!?' She tried to wake him but he was too tired. Melody pondered if the sandwich he'd eaten had been drugged. She ran to the window and in the darkness saw a figure entering a shed. Melody trembled and clamped her eyes as she slid down the wall.

Sunlight poured in from the curtains. There was a loud bang on the door and she awoke with a fright. She turned to check on Malcolm, but he was gone. Her heart pounded. She ran to the bathroom but he wasn't there. Melody scooped her belongings and dashed to the foyer. The pages of the guest book gusted in the wind.

"MALCOLM GRIFFITH – 23:00PM – IN"
"MALCOLM GRIFFITH – 08:00AM – OUT"

Dread pressed against her throat and she could feel herself wanting to cry. The door creaked open and Jan limped out.

'I hope you enjoyed your stay,' she fumbled. Melody trudged backwards outside. The buzzing of a chainsaw rattled the foliage and Andy emerged from the shed wielding it. She crouched in the weeds and muffled her breathing. A spider crawled over her toes and she bit her tongue to stop herself from screaming. Andy ventured back to the shed. Melody took her chance and sprinted into the woodlands. She desperately slapped the branches away from her face as she raced forwards. Finally she saw the highway and leapt onto it. She put her hands over her knees and took several breaths. The screeching of tyres filled the air as a car emerged from the muddy tracks. It blared its horn and surged after her. Her sandals slapped the asphalt as she ran, but the car eventually caught her. She peered over her shoulder and realized it was Malcolm. He opened the door and she crawled inside, desperately catching her breath.

'Mal… Malcolm… It's you…'

'Of course it's me. What are you doing? We were looking all over for you.'

'I'm sorry… I was so frightened. I thought something terrible happened,' she gasped.

He looked at her in the languid morning light.

'I told you everything would be fine… Why? What did *you think* was going to happen?'

The Prince

Long ago there existed an isle that housed a mountain of treasure. There was gold, silver, and dozens of sand-speckled crystals that glistened in the sunlight. One day, a young fisherman named Elon, found himself shipwrecked in a turbulent storm. Accompanied by his friends, Torres and Talleyrand, they quickly sought refuge on the isle. As Elon brushed the sand from his eyes, he couldn't believe his luck. He quickly woke his injured friends, and the trio jumped for joy, declaring themselves rich. Since Elon was captain at the time of discovery, he decided they share the treasure, and turn the peninsula into a prosperous kingdom.

Many years passed, and the trio who initially began life as lowly fishermen, were now prosperous and contented. One day, Elon decided that the kingdom needed a ruler and officials to govern society. A ballot was cast and by no surprise, the townsfolk unanimously voted him as their king. Elon graciously accepted, and wanting his friends by his side, he announced Torres as a general for the islands army, and appointed Tallyrand as his personal advisor. Elon ruled the kingdom in a peaceful manner, but as the years passed, numerous ailments eventually withered him. Now barely able to walk or converse, many deemed him unfit to rule. So one fateful day, his courtiers led by Torres and Tallyrand, marched upon the castle and seized the throne. Elon was executed and his family were banished to a far impoverished island. Fuelled by malice, Torres crowned himself king and ruled the kingdom uncontested. Like many of the tyrannical kings that preceded him, he had a penchant for cruelty. If you were alone in the castle and happened to whisper too loudly, or perhaps spill a glass of milk, he would likely have you beheaded, and you'd consider yourself lucky the king was in such a pleasant mood.

One day, the princess stumbled into the throne room. Out of all of the king's treasures, none was as sparkling as his daughter. She was the apple of his eye, and fortunately it had fallen very far from the tree.

'Dearest daughter, the time has come for you to be wedded!' The king's wine spilled from his cup as he roared. 'My lineage must carry the blood of a champion, and that requires challenge!'

Tallyrand stood tall beside him. He outstretched his bony fingers and whispered into the king's ear.

'Yes… perfect! We will test the challenger in mind, body, and sprit. If he is successful, I will offer your hand in marriage.'

'And what will happen if he loses?'

The king scratched his beard.

'If the challenger loses, a great peril shall await him!'

The princess went pale. 'But what happens if no one wins?'

Tallyrand's yellow teeth protruded as he snickered and whispered into the king's ear a second time.

'If no victor emerges, you will marry Tallyrand.

Although not my first choice, but it will secure our hold on the kingdom.'

The princess's throat swelled.

'Please father, this is barbaric! I beg of you…'

'Silence! 'The Trials of Torres' will commence at sunrise.'

It didn't take long for news to stretch over the land. Soon the kingdom was overrun with men of all ages from provinces afar. Many were courageous, but unfortunately none could best the trials.

On the furthest isle south of the kingdom, a lowly blacksmith named Elonso, walked home and counted his daily takings. As the sun crowned him in a golden warmth, he heard the ramblings of merchants reading from a scroll.

"You are cordially invited to 'The Trials of Torres.' If you are successful, you will have my daughter's hand in marriage - followed by an everlasting fortune to live your life in absolute merriment."

A snort of derision emerged on the townsfolk's faces. The merchants tossed the scroll to the dirt and Elonso curiously grasped it.

'Brother please! You must reconsider!?'

Elonso ignored his brother's pleas and continued packing a bundle of provisions for the journey.

'Do you seriously think you can win?'

Elonso carefully placed a bucket to catch the droplets of rain from the cracked roof.

'We can't keep living like this brother. We deserve so much more! And besides, they say she is the most beautiful in all the land...'

'But you can only capture her beauty if you win.'

'Yes and forbidden fruit is always the sweetest.'

Elonso flicked his black hair over his shoulder, and draped himself in a blue cloak. Embroidered on its back was their family crest.

'Mother passed this year too. I shall pray your name does not join her brother.'

Elonso closed his eyes momentarily.

'I will return brother, you have my word.'

Elonso leapt on his horse. The rain had cleared, and he galloped down the sunlit path as his brother chased after him.

'Elonso! You forgot your sword!'

'Keep it brother! The next time you see me,
I shall be a married man!'

By sunrise Elonso had reached the towering city gates. The sea breeze steadily wafted the aroma of wine and roasting nuts through the market. Elonso tied his horse to a nearby fence. Eyeing him was a merchant selling fresh fruit. There were dozens of merchants and traders in the sprawling market, but he was considerably old. His skin was the colour of parchment and wispy white hair curled behind his pointed ears.

'Ahh… you must be here to take on the trials?'

Elonso raised one eyebrow. 'How did you know?'

'I have seen many young men enter the kingdom of late. I pray for their safe passage, but unfortunately the castle is decorated with corpses of the damned.'

His voice revealed a hint of concern.

'You seem like a noble boy… Please take this!'

Rolling on his palm was a shiny red berry.

'Eat it… and may the Gods smile upon you.'

Elonso pinched it and examined it under the sunlight. 'What is it?'

'Miracle fruit,' said the old man.

Elonso smiled and safeguarded it in his breast pocket.

'How kind. I shall put it to good use!'

Elonso flicked his cloak over his shoulders and

walked towards the looming castle. As he approached the moat, the drawbridge suddenly ascended. Talleyrand appeared on the balcony and Elonso brandished the invitation. A glare of scorn reverberated around Talleyrand's cave-like eyes. Two guards appeared and escorted Elonso through the courtyard. Dozens of severed heads were displayed on pikes. Elonso grinned as a conspiracy of crows picked their decayed flesh. They led him up a winding staircase and halted outside a giant door. The brass bells atop the castle chimed. Elonso peered out the window as the residents of the kingdom stampeded into the courtyard. The door of the banqueting hall crashed open, and a long red carpet led to the throne. The king's eyes narrowed as the sunlight poured in. Elonso strode forward as a fanfare of trumpets blared, and dancing maidens threw rose petals at his feet.

'State your name!' roared the king.

Elonso's cloak fell over his shoulder as he bent the knee. The king curiously glared at the insignia.

'My name is Elonso.'

A pang of déjà vu struck the king. He stroked his beard, trying to ascertain why the boy looked familiar.

'So do you accept the challenge?'

'Yes, your majesty.'

'Let 'The Trials of Torres commence!'

The door slammed shut, plunging the room into darkness. The guards lit fiery torches and the crowd roared as Elonso scanned the arena.

'Wait! Where is the princess?' he inquired.

The king raised his giant hand. Atop him was a balcony with a red curtain. He clenched his fist and the curtains drew. Sitting down on a stool was the princess. Her hair was the colour of autumn leaves, and her soft blue eyes resembled broken mirrors. Elonso's gaze met with hers, but she quickly turned - nauseated from this barbaric exchange at her expense.

Talleyrand's nasal voice addressed the arena.

'Your first challenge will be none other than the fabled 'Trial by combat!'

The grim sound of clanking metal echoed around. Elonso peered over his shoulder. Behind him was a hefty warrior, coated in armour and wielding an axe.

'Ladies and gentlemen… The king's undefeated champion!' yelled Tallyrand.

Elonso grit his teeth, as the princess shielded her view with her hands.

'Pick one weapon from the table,' said the king.

'But your majesty, the low-born chose not to bring a weapon!' snarled Tallyrand.

'I arose early from my chambers for this unforeseen trial. I want to witness a bloodbath.'

Tallyrand reluctantly led Elonso to the table. Numerous weapons were on display. All jagged and designed for killing. Elonso chose a small dagger and scooped a handful of grapes from the fruit bowl. He squared up to the warrior and gave him some fruit.

'May the Gods smile upon you,' he declared.

They both ate and Elonso bowed to the king.

'Enough pleasantries! Begin!' he yelled.

The warrior swung his axe but Elonso swiftly ducked. The warrior swung a second time and managed to slash Elonso's face. The princess winced as speckles of blood dripped onto the floor. Elonso continued to duck and dodge, but this time the warrior cornered him. He raised his axe for a killing blow but suddenly dropped it. The warrior clasped his neck and blood spurted from his mouth. The king and princess rose up in awe as he mysteriously crashed down dead.

The crowd gasped and Elonso tossed the dagger back onto the table.

'What have you done to my champion?'

'My father once told me - "Beware of an old man, in a profession where most die young,' boasted Elonso.

'What are you talking about?' rasped Tallyrand.

'The old merchant in the market. He gave me fruit from the poisonous tree… so I fed it to your champion.'

The king sheepishly gestured with his hand, and two guards dragged the former champion away.

'This next trial will surely be your last!' taunted Tallyrand. 'Now we shall test your wisdom. Let's see how you fair against me! I am the smartest in the land. My intelligence begins where yours peaks!'

He clicked his fingers and two guards placed an overflowing treasure chest on the table.

'You may take **one item** from the table and present it to the king, but anything you ask for will be given to me in twofold. **If I accept what has been offered, you lose**… but if I decline then you will win.'

Tallyrand slithered back toward the throne.

'Proceed!'

Elonso hesitantly walked to the table. He ran his fingers across some gold coins.

'Ahh, the coin of the realm! Thank the Gods I was not born a miser!'

Elonso grit his teeth and pinched a diamond.

'Ooh! A diamond, offer the king one, and he will grant me with two! A fool I would be to decline!'

Elonso wiped the sweat from his forehead and glared at the fruit bowl.

'I will gladly accept fruit too!' snickered Tallyrand.

The crowd became restless and began to chant.

'Make your decision!' yelled the King.
Elonso's eyes darted and he reluctantly grasped the dagger again. He walked toward the king and brandished the weapon. The princess peered through her fingers as Tallyrand gleamed.

'You think I won't accept this pitiful dagger? I shall gladly have two daggers at the expense of your life!'

Elonso cleared his throat.

'Your majesty, please take this dagger… and use it to gouge but just **one** of my eyes.'

The arena fell silent. Talleyrand's face drained of

49

colour. The king turned to him slowly.

'No! I decline! Your majesty wait…'

'So you decline Tallyrand?'

'Of course! My vision is vital for the success of the monarchy!'

The king paused and pondered. He gestured with his hand and two guards swiftly disarmed Elonso. Just as Talleyrand's face beamed with joy, the guards seized his gangly arms and dragged him to the dungeons.

'Your majesty please! This is an absurdity!' Small veins appeared on the king's head as the crowd and princess cheered for Elonso. He continued to sneer at the insignia on Elonso's cape.

'Enough of this! Who are you?'

Elonso flicked his hair from his face.

'My name is Elonso.'

'Do not insult my memory, why do you look familiar?'

Elonso closed his eyes. 'I look familiar… because my father was the former king.'

The crowd gasped and the princess rose up in awe.

'It is destiny's wish that I will win,' declared Elonso.

The crowd began chanting and the king grit his teeth.

'Silence! Prepare the arena for the final trial!'

Elonso's eyes met with the princess again. This time, a faint smile appeared on her pursed lips. The king clapped his hands. Two guards blindfolded Elonso and removed him from the arena. The princess wailed over the balcony, and a piercing roar reverberated across the castle. The guards soon returned him and removed his blindfold. Elonso peered around. Strands of orange fur were nestled in the carpet, and opposite him were two large doors; both identical in appearance and approach. The princess stood beside the king - her face now void of all hope.

'Seeing as you're so fond of destiny, your final challenge will be the legendary 'Trial of the Gods!' Two doors stand before you. Behind one is a solid gold ring. You may use this ring to wed my beloved daughter. But behind the other door… is a man-eating tiger. Choose incorrectly and death is certain! Do not attempt to wait for a growl, because no sound shall pass through these impenetrable doors. So make your decision. What will it be? The lady or the tiger?'

Elonso eyed the princess who now stood opposite. She flashed an anxious glance, which halted fleetingly toward her left. No one but Elonso saw, as everyone's gaze was fixated upon him.

The room fell silent. All that could be heard was the cawing of crows upon the castle roof. Elonso stood tall, his blue eyes shone bright despite the shade of the arena. And so, the unsung prince of undoubted rank stepped up and opened… the right door.

Ace In The Hole

'Do you think I should thank God Susan?'

Too immersed in her book, she ignored him. Lawrence marched over and glanced at the cover in disdain.

"Little Women" what hokum are you reading now?'

'It's actually a gripping coming of age drama, you should read it.'

'Pah! Perhaps if I was the last person in the universe!'

Susan shut the book and rolled her eyes.

'What were you saying?'

Lawrence flinched as he failed to strap his bow tie.

'When I win the award tonight, I was thinking of ending the speech with…' Lawrence puffed his chest.

'I will work ever harder, as I firmly believe certainty is the enemy of science!' He enunciated his arms like a news anchor as Susan zipped her black evening gown.

'That's nice darling, but… what if you don't win?' His laugh, akin to a failing car engine filled the room.

'Who deserves it more than I Susan? Whom? Ahh I have it…' He clicked his fingers repeatedly. 'You think Dr. Fairfax will steal the award don't you? I should have known. You've always been in her corner.'

Susan scrunched her face.

'I had coffee with her, once! While I waited for your lecture to finish… I thought she was nice.'

'Pah! Don't be so easily fooled Susan. I know she plagiarized my groundbreaking thesis on molecular dynamics. Once a thief, always a thief.'

Lawrence crumpled the bow tie in his fist.

'To think a man of my stature, who can solve vast riddles within our universe, can't fathom the rubric of a lowly bow tie!'

A red carpet led toward the Nobel Institute. Camera shutters snapped as Lawrence and Susan strolled past the Norwegian press.

'Ah look, there's Dr. Fairfax,' muttered Susan.

The vein on Lawrence's forehead could not be suppressed. A cheer echoed from the crowd as she posed for the cameras.

'Are you coming to the bar Lawrence?' asked Susan. He continued to sneer at Dr. Fairfax on the red carpet.

'Lawrence! Are you coming for a drink?'

'No! You go ahead...'

Lawrence dashed to the toilet and splashed cold water over his face. After he composed himself, he sat by the bar and rehearsed his award speech.

'I'd like to thank God, my lovely wife Susan, and last but not least, the Nobel Institute, for making this dream a reality. I will work ever harder, as I firmly believe; certainty is the enemy of science!'

'I couldn't agree more,' said a voice from a behind.

He flinched and spun around. Dr. Fairfax stood proud behind him. She was a few inches taller with heels on, and was sporting a polka dot dress with white gloves. Lawrence upturned his nose at her garish outfit.

'I know... I look different without my lab coat, but its not often we get to dress up. And besides, there's a high probability I could even win.'

'A drop of sweat trickled from Lawrence's forehead and fell into his champagne glass.

'Pah! The Norwegians are saying the award is mine to lose. I mean when was the last time someone created a habitual planet in our solar system?'

'Perhaps, but don't disregard my vaccine for the cold and flu. Do you know how many lives I've saved? Think of the children Lawrence?'

'Oh I am, because one day they'll play hop scotch and take moon-selfies on my planet "Kraven 7."

'Well may the best man or woman win.'

Susan approached with a twenty something girl. She was wearing a red dress and her forearms were covered in tattoos.

'Susan! So lovely to see you!' exclaimed Dr. Fairfax.

'I see you've met my daughter,' she added. She smiled at the group. 'Anyway we better go find our seats, best of luck to you all!'

Lawrence gulped down his champagne.

'Aw! Her daughter was so lovely,' said Susan.

'Her arms look like a school detention desk.'

'What's come over you lately?'

'Always look at the mother before idolizing the daughter Susan. And speaking of Dr. Fairfax, what is she wearing? This is a prestigious event for scientific advances, it's not the Met Gala!'

The auditorium was at full capacity. Floral decorations covered the walls, and scientists from across the globe gave enthralling speeches. The lights dimmed and the guards on the upper balcony blared their trumpets as the host walked to centre stage.

'Ladies and gentlemen, the time has finally come. We will now introduce this evenings Nobel laureates.'

A screen in the foreground displayed pictures of Lawrence and Dr. Fairfax - along with their accolades. The host flourished a golden envelope and Lawrence closed his eyes as the orchestra produced a drum roll.

'And the 2030 Nobel Prize goes to… Dr. Franziska Fairfax!'

Lawrence snapped out of his trance. A thick phlegm formed in his throat, as Dr. Fairfax took the stage.

'… I would just like to thank my hero Marie Curie, and I will continue to work ever harder, as I firmly believe certainty is the enemy of science!'

Her eyes met with Lawrence and the faintest of smiles formed on her pursed lips. The crowd erupted in applause. Lawrence's fingernails ripped into the fabric of the armrest, and Susan kept a close eye on the vein on his temple, which was beating like a heart.

'I created a fucking planet Susan!' he yelled as the taxi drove them back to the hotel.

Lawrence stormed around the room like a raged toddler. He felt like the Nobel institute had removed his brain and hurled it against a wall.

'And she stole my line... Mark my words, she'll pay.'

Lawrence stepped out onto the balcony. The faint wisps of the aurora borealis speckled the night sky. He lit a cigarette and admired his planet - Kraven 7 – which was a speck in the distance. As he exhaled, a smile evolved on his face, a smile so wide it pushed his cheekbones into his eyelids.

'Yes... that's it! That's exactly what I'll do! Certainty is the death of the science, and soon Dr. Fairfax... it will be the death of you!'

When Susan awoke the next morning, Lawrence was nowhere to be seen. There was a note on the pillow - explaining he'd taken a redeye flight back to

London. When she eventually arrived home, the sound of clanking metal greeted her as she opened the door. She crept downstairs into the basement. Nuts and bolts were scattered everywhere and bursts of heat from a blowtorch singed her eyelashes. Lawrence took off his mask. He popped a cigarette in his mouth and used the blowtorch to light it. 'It's almost finished Susan.'

'What's almost finished?'

'My magnum opus.'

'Is this why you left early? So you could scheme in the darkness?'

'Pah! I won't be the one in the "darkness" Susan.' He smirked and polished the machine. It was shaped like a giant seesaw, with a narrow turret atop. Susan peered closer. Inside the centre was a dark rock.

'Don't go near that!' he yelled.

'What is this Lawrence? What have you done?'

'It's just a piece of uranium.'

'Uranium?!'

'Yes Susan, uranium! Now leave me be.'

The following morning, a seismic bang ruptured the entire house. Susan was hosting her fortnightly book club, and the entire group stared petrified, as the windows smashed around them. Lawrence emerged from the basement. His hair was frizzed and Susan's friends hastily exited.

'What was that?!' she asked.

He picked up the copy of "Little Women" and snarled.

'You'll see soon enough.'

◆

Dr. Fairfax peered through the telescope.

'Hmm that is strange… I wonder what's causing all those cyclones?' she muttered.

'If my calculations are correct, the discovery may bestow us as Nobel laureates for a second time. I'd be honored if you joined me for my research?'

Dr. Fairfax withdrew her Nobel Prize medal and polished it with her sleeve. 'When you put it like that Lawrence, how could I say no?'

After two days of flying, the self-piloted rocket landed on Kraven 7. A turbulent ion storm wrecked the atmosphere. Lawrence and Dr. Fairfax stepped out of the ship and onto the red sandy ground.

She gazed in wonderment, admiring the numerous cacti

and small ponds of water. Lawrence attached a safety wire to their spacesuits, which led back to the rocket.

'The activity seems to be coming from that ridge, let's head over,' he declared.

Gravity increased as they climbed a steep valley, and behind the orange mesas, Earth was a tiny dot in the distant. Whilst Dr. Fairfax admired the vista, Lawrence secretly cut the wire on her spacesuit.

'According to my coordinates, we should find the source at the peak, said Lawrence as he pointed to a narrow path. 'After you,' he added.

They were extremely high up, and the sudden force of gravity forced them to trudge. Dr. Fairfax tiptoed to the precipice and carefully peered over.

'Lawrence I don't believe it! It's a…'

But before she could respond. Lawrence pushed her into the black hole. She screamed as Lawrence's hollow laugh echoed across the galaxy. The black hole was the size of a basketball, but it was devastatingly powerful. Lawrence grinned as Dr. Fairfax stretched and extended like toothpaste forced from its tube. A loud snap echoed from her spine, and she was painfully extruded through the dark chasm.

Lawrence dusted his hands and skipped back to the rocket. As he went through his bag, he realized Susan had left him a copy of "Little Women." I hope the Martians need toilet paper he thought.

Eager to return home and start a thesis on black holes - he punched in the coordinates for earth. But a flicker in the reflection of his space helmet caught his attention. His eyes dilated and his face almost spilled off his skull. A huge asteroid with similar stature to a football stadium hurtled toward earth. By the time his jaw dropped it had decimated the entire planet. A rupture of light engulfed the cosmos and a hollow hum pervaded the nebula. Lawrence sat on a jagged rock, and a single tear fell down his eye as he gazed at the book. Suddenly he recalled what he'd said days prior.

'… You should read it.'

'Pah! Perhaps if I was the last person in the universe!'

Relegated to planetary confinement, Lawrence sighed and started reading.

"Christmas won't be Christmas without any presents," he grumbled.

The Lights Are On
But Nobody's Home

I always used to scoff at ghost stories.
I'm different now. Sometimes you see things, or go to places that make you think we honestly don't know what's out there. I guess the paranormal is under no obligation to define itself? Or maybe some places aren't meant to be scanned by human eyes?

Well I'll tell you what happened, I just hope I have enough time… Last year just before spring I divorced my husband. I was fortunate enough to get sole custody of my five-year-old son, Noah. As long as I saw a court ordered therapist, once a week for "psychological evaluation." As you can imagine, these sessions coupled with lawyer fees, were and still are a huge dent in my finances. Anyway… I took a job as a property guardian for a derelict apartment block. I needed the money and a temporary new home. So after researching the place online, I discovered a terrible accident befell there many years ago. The police never found the missing kids or the culprit. The strange thing was, according to the reports, there were no irregularities. No fingerprints, no murder weapon - the children simply went missing. It didn't take long for rumors to spread. Eventually people just avoided residing there entirely. Soon after, an oil tycoon bought the apartment complex. He planned to renovate the area into a bustling shopping centre, but until then, someone had to watch over the vacant building.

The Easter break had just started, and I remember it was raining as I dragged my suitcase from the taxi. Noah's tiny mouth gasped when he saw just how tall the high-rise building was. Before you ask… yes he was happy to be there, and yes he was happy to be with his mother finally. He was slightly withdrawn the night before, but you know how kids are at that age.

In fact I distinctly remember him running up the concrete steps, so he must've been somewhat excited for his new home. I held his hand as we walked through the entrance. A security concierge was asleep in a chair. He was an elderly oriental man. The elevator suddenly dinged and he awoke in fright. I turned around. No one emerged and the elevator doors slowly closed.

'Oh don't worry, it does that sometimes…'

I watched him fumble through paperwork on the desk. He rearranged his glasses as he read a document.

'You must be Janelle?'

He put on his coat and walked around the desk. Moments before handing me a key, he stared at Noah and pulled a ghastly face.

'Oh… you have a child?'

'Yes, this is my son, Noah.'

'Oh I see… you do know about the…'

'I'm aware of the history of this place, yes.'

He continued to stare with a mortified expression. I ushered Noah behind my leg and he slowly handed me the key.

'I suggest locking the front doors at all times. Also, you must check every hallway every night before you retire.'

'Really? I have to check all seven floors?'

'Well six actually, the elevator no longer goes to the seventh.'

The key indicated my room was on the sixth floor.

'Can I not have a ground floor room?'

'No… that is the only room which is worthy.'

'So I don't get a master key?'

He grit his teeth and scrunched his face.

'There is no master key. Well there was, but it went missing.'

'Went missing or someone stole it?'

'No. It went missing. Don't worry; you're the only occupant in this building… Well if you need anything else my number is on the desk. Farewell.'

I led him outside and that's when I saw it for the first time… One of the lights on the high-rise window turned on. I squinted and brushed the raindrops from my eyes, but the light had turned off. I thought nothing of it, and headed back inside. My gaze darted to the mailboxes on the wall. Most were empty and some were hoarding pizza takeaway leaflets, but in the bottom corner slot, nestled in tightly, was a child's stuffed bear. It was a dirtied white - like a child had dragged it through a muddy puddle.

'Can we take it?' asked Noah.

'No, leave it alone.'

I bit my nails as I stared at it. The elevator dinged again, and I turned around in shock, but it was just Noah who called for it. I grabbed my suitcase and we walked inside. Cigarette butts cushioned my shoes against the metal floor and a dim light flickered above. I watched Noah jump and attempt to press the button for the sixth floor. Although he couldn't reach them, he'd grown so much and I reminisced about his childhood.

I pressed the sixth floor button and the elevator screeched as we ascended. I always despised elevator mirrors, but this one unnerved me tenfold. The flicking light that kept distorting my reflection into a silhouette didn't help much either. Ding! The doors opened. The carpet was creaky and when the doors closed, it threw us into complete darkness. I smiled as Noah cleverly used the light on his iPad to guide us.

'Here we are, room 67.'

I opened the door and the meek afternoon light poured over my face. The rooms felt more spacious due to the numerous mirrors, and the fake plants doted on the tabletops did nothing to extinguish the foreboding aura. To be honest, I don't blame people for leaving. Why stay in a place if something harrowing happened within its walls?

I poured myself a glass of water, but halted before I sipped. The water was cloudy like pond water. I tossed it down the sink and checked on Noah to see if he liked his room. When I opened the door, he was sat on the bed, hunched over and snickering. He wasn't playing with his iPad because it was on the bed. I dashed over to see what he was laughing at. 'Noah?'

He ignored me so I physically turned him.

'What are you doing?'

He dropped the stuffed toy bear to the floor. My stomach muscles clamped as I grabbed it. The feel of its dirtied moist cotton on my fingertips really disturbed me. 'Where did you get this?'

I grabbed his face so he knew I was serious.

'Answer me!'

'I found it under the bed…'

'Don't lie. I specifically told you not to touch this!'

'I'm not lying! It was under the bed.'

I checked under the bed. Nothing else was there. I realized his attention was on back on the bear. It irked me so I held it behind my back.

'Don't take things that don't belong to you. Okay?'

He puffed and picked up his iPad. I knew the divorce had been tough on him, so I didn't want to scold him. I went to the kitchen and hid the toy in one of the high cupboards. Then I pulled out my phone and ordered a Chinese. About thirty minutes later I got a message on my phone. I told Noah I wouldn't be long and left the apartment. I wanted to lock the door from the outside, but refrained. As a mother you always assume the worst in situations like that. Do you have kids? It's like when the schoolteacher rings, and you instantly assume your child's broke their neck on the jungle gym, or a fire will magically break out in the house… Anyway I didn't lock him inside. I walked down the hallway. The red light atop the elevator indicated it was on the seventh floor. That was the exact moment the lump formed in my throat.

How did it get there? And who called for it?   Ding!
I hushed my breathing. I was certain I heard footsteps
from above tap the ceiling. Suddenly it descended to
the ground floor. My stomach tightened and I ran
down the staircase. My footsteps echoed across the
whole building as I raced to keep up. I finally reached
the reception and grabbed a pen as a makeshift weapon.
Ding! The doors opened, but jammed halfway. I
squinted and my grip around the pen tightened. Finally
they opened, but no one was inside. I laughed and
caught my breath.

When I got outside I apologized to the driver.

'I'm sorry; sometimes the elevator has a mind of its
own. I had to take the stairs.'

'That's fine. It seems like quite the journey.'

His remark threw me. 'What do you mean?'

He handed me the food bag and before he closed
his visor, he tilted his head up at the building. He sped
off and as the exhaust fumes cleared, I slowly turned.
My fingers lost their grip and I dropped the bag. The
light on the seventh floor was on again. My heart
thumped against my chest. I grabbed the bag and ran
inside. The elevator was awaiting me and the doors

were strangely open. I leapt inside and examined the buttons. The seventh floor could only be accessed with a key. I hammered the sixth floor button and the elevator wailed as it ascended. When the doors opened the silhouette of a small child was in the hallway. In its grasp was the cuddly toy. I leapt back. My shoulder blades crashed into the door and my eyes adjusted to the darkness. It was Noah. I wiped the sweat from my forehead and carried him into the room.

'What on earth were you doing out there?'

I shook him out of his trance and glanced around the kitchen. All of the cupboard doors were open. I reprimanded him for not listening, but he continued to act strange and withdrawn. Nothing else happened that night, thank God.

I know what you're thinking… Why didn't I just up and leave? Because I literally had nowhere else to go. My sister lived on the other side of town so I thought, just stay the night, try and get some sleep and see how tomorrow pans out. When I look back on it now, I should have left that very night...

The next morning I took a shower. I remember it vividly because the drain was clogged with jet-black hair that wasn't mine. The water had a rotten smell too. It was unlike anything I'd ever smelt, even worse then the smell of wet dog. It lingered on my skin too, like after you regretfully dry yourself with a damp towel.

We didn't do much during the day except a small food shop. Upon return, that uneasy feeling edged back into my throat when we approached the elevator. It was on the seventh floor again, but this time, it refused to descend. Noah helped me carry the bags up six flights of stairs. I realized too that the stairs stopped on our floor. So there was literally no access to the seventh floor without a key.

Shortly after I took a nap on the sofa, I woke up when loud footsteps thudded across the ceiling. They were so loud that the banal artwork on the walls started shaking. I ran into my room and realized the cuddly toy was missing again. I scrammed into Noah's room. His iPad was on the dresser playing cartoons but he wasn't there. The hairs on my neck stood and I dashed out the apartment screaming his name. I was in such a panic I didn't even bother with the blasted elevator. I was out of breath by the time I reached the reception, and my bare feet were cracked and bleeding from the concrete steps. It was dark but the streetlamps did enough to light the reception. I called the security guard's number. There was no answer so I left a message.

'This is Janelle! You have to come back! My son's missing. Please get here immediately!'

I turned to the mailboxes. The cuddly toy was still there. I scratched my head in confusion and pulled it out. On its underside was a zipper. The inside was fluffy and something was perched inside. I grasped my fingers tightly and withdrew a long rusted key.

I cautiously walked to the elevator. It was still on the seventh floor, but the doors mysteriously opened to reveal a dangerous empty shaft. I made sure to grip the wall before peering inside. A cold wind gusted my hair and I glared down into the abyss. Something was down at the very bottom. It looked like the mangled body of a child. My breathing became erratic. I leaned forward but could no longer see it. Suddenly the cables jolted. I yanked my head before the elevator bludgeoned me. I caught my breath as the doors opened. The key was a perfect fit and the elevator rattled as it ascended to the seventh floor. It came to a halt and I crept out.

The doors closed and threw the hallway into complete darkness. My bare feet touched the moist carpet and I instantly regretted not wearing shoes. All I could hear was my breathing and the squeaking of mice. A narrow rectangular light was coming from underneath one of the doors. I scrunched my face so the cobwebs wouldn't enter my mouth and kept going. The door creaked open and the stench overpowered me. It was like someone had sprayed a corpse with cheap perfume. I tucked my nose into my shirt as I crept into the living room. The wallpapers were ripped and mould was leaking out of them like pus. I called for Noah but didn't get an answer. I wandered into the broken skeleton of a child's bedroom. It was much colder than the rest of the apartment, coupled with a sinister aura, like it was lamenting something tragic. I know you want me to elaborate, but I really can't. It was just odd. A dusty photo was on the dresser. It was a girl, roughly the same age as Noah. Her circular face was malnourished, and patchy black hair fell from her shoulders. She was sitting on the bed surrounded by cuddly toys. In her hands was the white bear. I looked closer and realized her arms and legs were discoloured.

The contrast of bruises and stuffed animals made me wince. It was deathly silent until the elevator dinged. I dropped the photo and ran outside. The doors were open but it was just the empty shaft. I squinted and spotted Noah walking towards it holding the bear. I screamed his name as he peered over the edge. I sprinted towards him and grabbed him before he fell down the shaft. I shook him hard to snap him from his trance. That's when I noticed the bruises on his body. I know he bruised easily because he was always tumbling around, but these marks were identical to the girl's bruises in the photo. When he opened his eyes, he had this bizarre look on his face - like he couldn't remember who I was. I scooped him up and realized he wouldn't let go of the bear. For the life of me I couldn't remove it from his grasp. The elevator appeared and I knew we needed to get out of the building immediately. We scrammed inside and I repeatedly pressed the ground floor button. Suddenly one of the apartment doors creaked open. Light spilled into the hallway and the floorboards started to creak like someone was walking over them. My gut feeling was that something vengeful was among us. The elevator light violently flickered and I slammed the button again. The doors finally shut. But the elevator acted with a mind of its own and plummeted down. I held Noah as tight as I could. It abruptly halted and I smashed my head against the cold metal. The lights cut out and all I could hear was my erratic breathing. A cold breath moistened the back of my neck. I turned around as the lights switched on. I screamed so loud my tonsils went sore. In the reflection was a girl. Black hair fell across her pale face and my feet slid as I pushed myself into the corner and shielded Noah. Her hands ventured through the mirror and her cracked fingernails pierced my skin as she snatched the stuffed bear. I shrieked and repeatedly struck the ground floor button. Blood dripped from my knuckles as I kept smashing it. The lights flashed and the elevator jolted down. She was no longer in the reflection. I slowly rose to my feet as the doors opened and realized the cuddly toy was gone. I checked Noah's face but his eyes were clamped shut. The lights flashed and a crowbar pried open the door. I leapt back but it was just the security guard. He comforted us and called for an ambulance shortly after…

Noah says he can hardly remember any of it now. I wish I could say the same for myself. To this day no one really believes me. The police certainly didn't… and don't get me started on the child welfare services. In fact, it wouldn't surprise me if you're ascribing me with some "meta" prognosis - "It was just your grief hallucinating the divorce."

'That's certainly not what I'm thinking Janelle.'

She raised her eyebrow and took a sip of water.

'So Janelle, how has the experience changed you?'

I took a deep breath and stared at the numerous certificates on her office wall.

'Well I currently have a fear of looking in mirrors, can you blame me? And as far as elevators are concerned… let's just say now I always take the stairs.'

Only God Forgives

'We shall end today's sermon with the eternal advice from "Luke: 27 – 29: Love your enemies, do good to those who hate you, bless those who curse you. pray for those who mistreat you. Whoever hits you on the cheek, offer him the other."'

Godiva lit two candles as Father Andrew greeted her.

'Who are they for if you don't mind me asking?'

'Just my two dogs…'

He clasped her hands and smiled.

'It's lovely to see you Mrs. Holland, although I'd much prefer if you attend morning mass. The petty crime seems to have fallen but its still...'

'Morning mass?! Lord knows I can't miss the bingo Father! Don't you worry, those thugs can't hold a battle-axe like me!'

Father Andrew blessed her and bided her farewell.

It was a cold sharp night and the streets were empty. Godiva peered around to make sure no one was following her. She removed her pearl necklace and placed it in her handbag. Home was just a stones throw away and the tapping of her heels reverberated across the dimly lit street. However as she readied her house keys, a hand suddenly covered her mouth and dragged her into an alleyway. Sharp fingernails dug into her gums and the cold metal of her zipper jacket pressed into her chin as she desperately tried to wrestle to safety. The hand pressed harder into her face, and in the scramble her handbag snapped. The perpetrator snatched it, but before escaping, Godiva withdrew her pepper spray and spritzed him in the eyes. His scream pierced the air and he clattered into the lamppost, like a badly driven remote control car.

'That's what you get for assaulting Godiva Holland-Carter!' she proclaimed as she snatched her handbag.

Godiva clipped him around the ear.

'Stop rubbing your eyes. You'll only make it worse!' She grabbed his chin and inspected his skeletal face under the cone of light.

'My goodness… How old are you?'

'Old enough you fat bitch!'

Godiva gasped so loudly the mice dashed back into hiding. 'What business do you have with my purse?!'

'Money.'

'Why?'

'Food.'

The flashing blue lights of a police car illuminated the alleyway. The boy kissed his teeth.

'Do you really need money for food?'

'Yes.'

'Not drugs or alcohol?'

'No, food.'

Godiva put her hands on her hips.

'A good home cooked meal is what you need boy.'

He kissed his teeth.

'It's not a choice young man. I'm going to set you straight. You're coming home with me right now or I'll hand you to the police myself.'

Godiva dragged him by the ear.

'What's your name?'

'... Ripper.'

Godiva gasped again. 'Don't lie to me boy!'

'It's what they called me prison.'

'Well you're not in prison anymore!'

'Kevin. Okay? You happy?'

'Well now we're getting somewhere.'

Godiva opened the door and led him to the kitchen. Kevin sniffed the air. The house had a perennial smell of broth, even though none was being made. He took a seat on the circular kitchen table and scrunched his face at the numerous tins of dog food. Godiva suddenly brandished a large knife and turned to him. Kevin instantly put his arms up in shock.

'Oh my apologies... here peel these,' she said and tossed him a clove of garlic.

He dug his fingers into the clove and Godiva clipped him around the ear again.

'Boy have you lost your damn mind? Wash your hands now... with soap!'

Kevin puffed and cleaned up in the sink.

'So are you going to apologize for earlier?' she asked.

He kissed his teeth as he peeled the garlic.

'Excuse you? Would you like me to call the police and explain why you're here?'

She picked up her phone and initiated a call.

'Okay! Jeez… I'm sorry.'

There was a loud stomp from upstairs. The frying pan hissed as Godiva quickly tossed in the garlic.

'I saw you come out of the church,' he muttered.

'That's right, every Sunday evening.'

'But if people don't sin, Jesus died for nothing.'

'Boy what kind of misguided thinking is that?'

'It's what someone said to me in prison.'

'Well if you heard it in prison, take it with a boulder of salt, and on that note, could you pass it to me? Second drawer on the right.'

As he grabbed the salt dispenser, another loud stomp echoed from the ceiling.

'What is that?' he asked.

'I have a few dogs.'

Kevin scrunched his face.

'How come they didn't come to the door?'

'Because I've trained them well.'

His nose twitched as he smelt the large pot.

'Why are you doing this?' he asked.

'Father Andrew once told me… "Sometimes we fail to realize we hold the key to our own prisons." That being said, maybe certain people deserve a second chance. Do you think you deserve one?'

'Yeah course.'

Godiva glared daggers into him. She scooped some rice and poured an ample amount of chili over it.

'Go on now, eat before it gets cold.'

Kevin tucked in and smiled.

'See, a home cooked meal always hits the soul.'

'Thank you… Mrs. Carter.'

'You're welcome… So what do you plan on doing with yourself?'

'A friend of mine works in the local garage. I've always been good with my hands. That's actually how I got in this mess… I fell in with a bad crowd and got roped in to stealing cars. It was a few days after my eighteenth birthday, so they tried me as an adult. But like you said, everyone deserves second chances.'

'No… I said "certain people" deserve them.' Godiva scooped some chili, but accidentally spilled some on her dress. She patted herself with a napkin then scurried to the bathroom. Her bag was unattended on the table and Kevin eyed it like a vulture. He slowly put down the spoon and clawed through it. As he pocketed her pearl necklace, Godiva's pepper spray bottle rolled onto the floor. He quickly grabbed it and concealed it in his fist. Godiva soon returned and he immediately returned the bag.

'Well I better be on my way,' he mumbled.

'What so soon?'

Kevin coiled his fingers around the nozzle of the pepper spray.

'Yeah, it's best I get an early night. The garage opens early tomorrow.'

'Okay well, let me just grab something for you...' Godiva reached inside her handbag.

'I want to give you Father Andrew's card, if you ever find yourself in trouble again, I want you to call him... That's strange... I'm sure it was right here. Maybe I left it in my purse?'

Kevin readied his finger on the trigger. Godiva looked up in confusion. He kissed his teeth and pressed his finger on the trigger.

'Oh my, the others only took the money and pearls,

but you took the spray too,' she said unblinkingly.

Kevin's eyebrows contorted in confusion. Godiva pulled out the real pepper spray and spritzed him a second time. He wailed and crashed into the fridge. Godiva kissed her teeth and repeatedly thrashed him with a frying pan until he slumped over the table.

When Kevin woke, his hands and legs were tied and he felt his head thud against the staircase. Constant banging echoed from two adjacent doors in the hallway. Godiva opened a tin of dog food and emptied its contents into a dog bowl.

'Settle down boys, dinners ready. Today's Sunday, so that means Lamb… with jelly chunks!'

Godiva slid the dog bowl through an opening. She pulled out a small key and unlocked another door.

'Make yourself comfortable Kevin,' said Godiva as she tossed him inside and locked the door.

Before retiring for bed, Godiva refastened her pearl necklace and grinned as she read from her bible.

"Do not give dogs what is holy, and do not throw your pearls before pigs, lest they trample them underfoot and turn to attack you." Matthew 7:6

Yesterday Was Beautiful

Kennedy buried his face in the pillow. His ears could no longer disregard the birds chirping on the cabin roof. He grimaced as he clambered out of bed and trudged to the window. The mountain mist had enveloped the distant metropolis, and the green hillsides lay back against the blue sky. Moments from opening the window, he quickly halted.

He limped down the wooden stairs. The gas masks, which hung upon the front door, were a sorrowful reminder of the bleak situation. Kennedy yanked open the fridge and scowled. Rose, his wife of almost fifty years, was preparing breakfast in the kitchen.

'Morning, did you sleep well?' she asked.

He bit the bottle cap off a beer then chugged it down. Rose shook her head. 'That's your breakfast?'

'American heart, Irish blood, Russian liver,' he snickered.

He fell back into his chair and remnants of beer splashed onto his vest. Rose stared in disdain as he licked it clean. A special news report was on TV and she turned up the volume.

"Today marks one year since the asteroid struck the Black sea. Due to the noxious hydrogen sulfide cloud - which formed thereafter, we'd like to remind everyone to stay indoors and seal your windows. If no masks are available – do not stay outside for longer than **five minutes** – we repeat do not…'

Kennedy changed the channel.

'I was watching that!' yelled Rose.

'Nothing but fear mongering.'

'But there could be an update, what if…'

'Update? It's the same goddamn thing everyday.'

'Let's pray they find a cure soon; it's our fiftieth anniversary next month. Wouldn't it be nice to go dancing like we used to?'

Kennedy sneered at the thought.

'There is no cure. Let the weak perish… or as we used to say in the trenches – "Only the strong will continue."

Rose crouched beside him and placed her hand over his. 'What happened to you Kennedy?'

Kennedy belched and shoved the empty beer bottle into her hands.

'Do your job and get me another drink.'

Rose clamped her eyes and sighed.

'Sometimes I think the only thing worse than the virus is you,' she muttered as she left the room.

◆

Kennedy awoke to the sound of rain. The beer bottles around his desk reflected the flashes of lightning from the skylight above. He turned on his computer. The grandfather clock struck midnight and its bell chimed across the lonely attic. A video call abruptly commenced and he scrambled to put on his glasses. The picture quality was distorted, but Kennedy gleaned it was a young girl wearing a military uniform. Her small nose was smattered with freckles, and a bright red rose was perched in her brown hair.

'Who are you?' he enquired.

'My apologies sir! I have the wrong connection.'

'This website is for veterans only. It's for us to trade stories and reconnect. It's not for punk kids.'

The young girl twitched at his flippant remark.

'First of all sir, I'm a military nurse, and I can ask you the same thing. This service is for military personnel only!'

Kennedy's turned crimson, but his anger subsided when the sound of gunshots blasted around the attic.

'What's all that noise?!'

The girl winced and flicked the debris from her hair.

'This war is terrible, I pray it will be over soon.'

'Is this some twisted joke?'

Small wrinkles appeared on the girl's forehead.

'No sir, I wanted to contact my friend. She's a nurse too, but stationed miles away.'

'Wait… what war exactly?'

'WW3 - The Crimean Revolt sir.'

Kennedy squeezed his dog tags in his fist.

'What are you talking about?! We won that war!
I was a Captain for the Crimean army. Twice
decorated! Let me show you my medals.'

He abruptly stood, however the sound of a bomb
blast echoed from beyond the screen.

'Oh no! I have to go. It was nice meeting you!'

'No… wait!'

The call ended and Kennedy scratched his head in
disbelief.

◆

The fumes from Kennedy's cigarette forced Rose to
cough.

'Must you smoke at the dinner table?'

He stubbed the cigarette on his tongue, and
pierced the chicken with his fork.

'Why is it so stale?'

Rose ignored him and sipped her water.

'I asked you a question. Answer me.'

'Because you left all the food in the delivery box!
Funny how you didn't forget to bring in the alcohol.'

'Alcohol numbs the sound of your nagging voice.'

Tears fell from her eyes as she dropped the cutlery.

'Kennedy, when this is all over I suggest you find someone else to put up with you…'

After dinner, Kennedy aimlessly sat by the computer. Another thunderstorm ravaged the sky and at exactly midnight another call started automatically. It was the mysterious girl. This time, the sleeves of her medical coat were rolled to her elbows, and another red rose was perched in her hair. There was something alluring about her; so much so that a smile unraveled on Kennedy's shrapnel scarred face.

'Oh no! Sorry to bother you again sir, I'll leave…'

'No it's fine. Please stay… You look lovely today.'

A smile emerged on her face.

'That's kind of you sir. Please excuse my memory, but what did you say you use this service for?'

'This video service was setup to aid veterans suffering from PTSD after the war.'

She scratched her head in confusion.

'After the war?'

'Yes. Why the long face?'

'Oh its nothing… well I have a few minutes, so what stories do you have to share?'

Kennedy sat up elated. 'Oh I can tell you dozens!'

◆

A month soon passed, and Kennedy found much joy conversing with her on a weekly basis. She was a mere twenty-three, but he loved recounting his numerous war stories, and imparting her with sage advice he'd accrued over the years. On this particular day, she was wearing an ethereal white dress, and as per usual she had placed a rose in her fringe.

'You know Kennedy… It's always been my dream to live by the mountainside, and dance in a moonlit field, surrounded by stars… And that's why it pains me to say this, but this will be my last transmission.'

Kennedy's throat swelled.

'But why? Where are you going?'

'Well the war is almost over, and my fiancé is soon to be discharged from duty. We're planning on moving to the mountainside so we can start a new life together.'

A sharp pain shot through Kennedy's heart.

'… Well I hope he takes good care of you.'

'Before I go, I just want to say, although you never believe me about who I am or where I'm from… I'm still grateful to have met you. I must go! Take care!'

'No wait!'

The grandfather clock struck midnight and the screen cut to black as she disappeared. Kennedy desperately shook the screen, but it was too late, the girl was gone.

Kennedy wandered around the attic like a lost child. He brushed aside cobwebs and withdrew an old chest, containing his uniform and medals. At the very bottom of his keepsakes was an antiquated photo of him and Rose on their anniversary. He ran his fingers over the frame, and his eyes widened as he blew away the dust. His hand jittered and the photo slipped from his grasp.

The medals on Kennedy's uniform jingled as he traversed down the wooden staircase. He removed the beer bottle atop the record player and played his wife's favourite song. Upon hearing the music, a flabbergasted Rose walked into the room. She was wearing an ethereal white dress with a rose in her fringe. A soft smile appeared on Kennedy's lips.

'Why are you wearing your military uniform?'
He extended his hand and Rose reluctantly grasped it.

'Kennedy, what are you doing?' she asked.

'Happy anniversary Rose.'

He whisked her to the front door. The gas masks fell as he opened it.

'Wait! We need the safety masks!'

He ignored her and set a timer on his watch.

'You heard the news. We have **five minutes**…'

Kennedy led Rose onto the green fields. A full moon adorned the night sky, and the music echoed across the mountaintops. He twirled her in the moonlight, and allowed the wind to gust her hair.

'I love you Rose,' he whispered.

He kissed her deeply, and the pair, framed by the fields and stars slow danced away.

The Falcon & The Viper

Once upon a time, deep in the heart of the African savannah, a war of unmatched scale and ferocity tore through the land. There are two sides to every story, and there were also two sides to the savannah.

If you were to sit in the shade of the acacia tree, the visage would shower you with a host of animals. Gazelles would dart across the sunbaked grass, flamingoes would soar across pink sunsets, and elephants, hippos, and zebras would quench their thirst in the huge watering hole. A fierce lion ruled over this region, and to many inhabitants he was known as the

"King of the Jungle." So powerful was his roar, it could create fissures in the earth and so strong was his bite it could crush the hardest of metals.

However, a few miles north of the watering hole was a brooding rainforest. Iridescent parrots sung from the treetops, sloths slept in the shrubs, and monkeys would use the branches to traverse the evergreen. Occupying the thoughts of these forest dwellers was one key notion. The gorilla was the true "King of the Jungle." He was a huge uncontested beast. A mere punch could topple an entire tree, and his jaws could disintegrate most into a fine powder.

One fateful day, the gorilla returned home to find one of his infants mauled to death. A smatter of golden hairs, resembling a lion's mane were dotted around her lifeless body. Seething with rage, he traversed to the watering hole and waited patiently until the lioness retreated. When her smallest cub came within reach, he violently clubbed him to death. Before venturing back to the forest, he pounded his chest for all the animals to see. One of those animals was a falcon, and he flew immediately to the lion's den to alert them of the tragedy. However upon arrival, he met with a snake -

the lion's best friend. The falcon informed him of the disaster, and the snake coiled inwards and regretfully broke the news to the lion. A ferocious roar echoed from the den as the lion demanded retribution.

From that moment on, a terrifying conflict emerged. Hundreds of animals lost their lives, and some unfortunate mammals became extinct. After months of torrid warfare, the snake, distressed with the sheer acts of violence, initiated a secret meeting between the two groups. Disguised as a banquet in honour of the lion's rule, he invited the entire savannah. Whilst everyone was at their most jovial, the snake led the gorilla and the rainforest dwellers into the den. The falcon had trailed the snake from afar, and he watched with suspicion from a safe vantage point.

The lion aimed his sharp claws at his best friend.

'How dare you betray me!?' he roared.

The snake slithered toward him.

'Oh lion, not a day goes by where I don't recall you saving my life from the dreaded mongoose. I present to you, the gorilla - leader of the rainforest. He wishes to quell the violence that has plagued our savannah.'

The lion savagely roared at the gorilla.

'First, explain the merciless killing of my cub?'

'Not until you confess to the murder of my offspring!' yelled the Gorilla.

The lion's eyes squinted in confusion and the snake anxiously inflated his hood.

'We must shed the skins of the past! The savannah has suffered enough!' he yelled.

The lion glared at the gorilla, but eventually offered his paw in forgiveness. The savannah fell silent, and after a moments thought, the gorilla accepted his peace offering. The snake sighed in relief and coiled up.

'Let us drink in honour of the mighty. To the lion and gorilla - 'Kings of the Jungle!'

He hissed in delight as all of the inhabitants drunk in merriment. However, it didn't take long until a petrifying cry shook the savannah. The animals fell in agony and the falcon quickly discerned their drinks had been poisoned with venom. As the lion and gorilla stood hesitant at the carnage, the snake seized his chance. He bore his fangs and crunched into the lion's neck – delivering a potent dose of venom. The gorilla's attempts to save his new friend were futile, as the snake savagely leapt on him and strangled him to death.

The serpent's calm blue scales converged into a blood red, and he reared up under the moonlight.

'To those who have survived, remember this moment, for it was I the snake who slayed the mighty!'

The falcon watched from above as all of the remaining animals knelt in fear.

'Falcon! You will become my winged messenger. Fly forth and alert the jungle they have a new king. For a name without fame, is fire without flame!'

◆

The chessboard of the savannah changed with the snake at the helm. Most animals lived in constant fear, and mammals that posed a threat, would be killed before maturity. Monkeys were recruited for security, and worms were used as his personal spies. And the fresh watering hole, once the crown jewel of the region, was envenomated with the snake's poison.

One day, the snake ordered an owl to rebuild the lion's den as his new home. The falcon warned his friend not to accept the offer, but overcome with pride, the owl refused to heed his advice.

'Oh falcon, once the viper king lays eyes on my glorious work, I will be coveted across the land.'

The Falcon shook his head.

'Help a serpent in kindness, and learn the limitations of kindness,' he warned.

When the owl finished his work, he covered the spectacle in palm leaves and invited the entire savannah. When the snake arrived, the owl unveiled his fabulous new den. The entrance resembled a giant serpent's head, leading to a cool mellow burrow. The snake's jaw dropped and the owl bowed to everyone in attendance.

'This is a fine den… but what a folly it would be if someone were to replicate it. Are you the only raptor who can compose such a design?' quizzed the snake.

'Indeed I am,' said the owl, as he looked at the falcon with a twinkle in his eye.

The snake slithered in front of him. 'No other shall share my design… Although I am indebted to you, gratitude is forever a burden but cruelty a pleasure.'

And with those words, the snake spat a vile venom into the owl's eyes, blinding him indefinitely. The falcon watched in despair as his hapless friend crashed into the trees, struggling to fly home. He cursed under his breath and vowed to rid the savannah of its tyrannical serpent.

◆

After a long hot summer, the snake grew bored of mundane jungle life.

'I have devised a new game,' he said to the falcon. 'At sunset, everyone must gather around the watering hole. I will then choose two animals to fight to the death! The loser will be thrown into the water where my venom shall corrode them. Now go forth and alert the savannah!'

Whilst the falcon flew high above the jungle, he spotted his brother, whom he had not seen for many years. They landed on a rock in the forest, and devised a cunning plan to thwart the viper's reign. However as they conspired, a solitary worm eavesdropped from the muddy terrain. No sooner had they departed, the worm wriggled with immediacy and alerted the snake of the conspiracy. At sunset, all of the animals nervously gathered by the watering hole. The snake, escorted by his monkey guards slithered to the front.

'Now we shall witness the survival of the fittest!'
He glared around the circle of timid animals and
unexpectedly hissed at the falcon.

'For your act of treason, you shall be punished!'
Before the stunned falcon could respond, the monkeys
seized him and threw him into a bamboo stick cage.

'Do you have any last words?' asked the snake.

The falcon hung his head in shame.

'Please travel to the jungle and announce my
captivity to my brother.'

Eager to witness his brother's misery, the snake
traversed to the jungle and called out to the treetops.

'Falcon! Your brother is soon to be killed!'

After a moment of silence, a lone falcon collapsed
from the sky and smacked the forest floor.

'Their foisted ploy must have shocked him to
death,' gloated the snake.

It was nightfall when the snake returned, and he
gleefully displayed his brother's carcass to the falcon.
Upon seeing his dead kinsman, the falcon dropped
dead to the bottom of the cage. The snake hissed.

'I have killed two birds with one stone!'

The snake opened the cage and bore his fangs.

But the falcon surprisingly sprung to life and seized him with breakneck speed. He crushed the viper with his sharp talons and shot towards the sky like an arrow from a bow. The snake desperately tried to wriggle free, but the falcon spiraled towards the rocky ground at a devastating pace. He then flung the snake so hard it shattered the ground - forming a huge crater upon impact. The falcon's brother rose from feigning death, and the entire savannah rejoiced over the snake's certain passing. As the falcon and his brother flew toward a new horizon, he uttered these final words.

'Crown a new worthy king, but forever consider, no matter how many times a snake sheds its skin, it is always still a snake.'

Encore

The collective gaze of the audience crawled over Hana like an unwanted lover. Sweat poured from the roots of her hair as she fumbled her lines centre stage. Her parents veiled their faces in shame, and the director sitting in the front row ripped his program. Blood surged to her face and she crashed to the floor.

Hana woke up in a fright. She swatted her face repeatedly. Her sheets were soaked in sweat and she flung them off her body. It was unusually warm for Japan in September and she opened the window. The moon hung above Mount Fuji like a paper lantern and from its position she knew it was late.

She poured some milk into a bowl and placed it on the windowsill for the stray cat to drink. Hana's feet were blistered from a twelve-hour shift at the restaurant. Eviction letters covered the fridge, as she swigged a concoction of painkillers and sleeping pills in her tiny kitchen. The red light was blinking on her voicemail and she hit play. Her fathers rasping voice filled the air.

"This is your last warning Hana. You haven't returned my calls in over a week. Your mother and I have decided not to lend you any more money, until you get a real job. Maybe now you'll realize..."

Hana deleted the message. Months had passed since her last fulfilling acting job, and having only just moved out, she was determined to make a name for herself in the acting world. Unfortunately, Hana had enough rejection letters to wallpaper her apartment in Fujiyoshida. Her eyes strained as she scoured the Internet, eagerly applying for acting jobs. Moments before retiring for the night, her laptop surprisingly buzzed. Hana scrunched her face. Who was emailing her at this hour? She trudged to the laptop and braced herself for the inevitable impact of "We regret to inform you..." However when she looked at the screen, sitting atop her inbox was a cryptic email. The subject line read.

"You're Perfect!"

Hana opened the email. "If interested, please respond to this emergency casting, and arrive at the Kitsune Theatre tomorrow morning at 9AM."

A hot flush ran through her body. The Kitsune Theatre was an infamous playhouse on the other side of town. Numerous actors claimed it was cursed, as decade's prior; an actress suffered a horrific injury on stage. Then during a subsequent showing, the theatre caught fire and burnt down. The sole survivor was the director. Hana carried her laptop to the open window, and languidly watched a fly crawl along the glass. She took a deep breath as her fingers danced across the keyboard. "Hi. I'll be there... Best wishes, Hana."

The next morning, Hana sipped her coffee and headed to the theatre. She finally stumbled across a derelict building with chipped paint. The faded insignia of a fox holding a theatre mask was engraved above the entrance. Hana knocked on the door. A fox suddenly leapt out of the nearby bin. She gasped and dropped her coffee. The white fur around its muzzle was covered in blood. She wanted to check if it was hurt, but it dashed away when she got near. Hana shuddered and knocked on the door again. There was no answer. Fearing she'd be late, she opened the door and crept down the gloomy stairs. She could only see as far as the blinking light bulb allowed, but a dusty sign indicated the stage was at the end of the hall. She heard people chattering and entered the nearest door.

'Refrain from telling her anything! We can't let her find out,' said a skinny man smoking a cigarette.

The man looked at Hana like she was a strange animal at the zoo. However she recognized him instantly. It was Satoru Nobu - a distinguished director known for his draconian approach with actors.
A plump woman wearing a facemask instantly stood. She held a clipboard with Hana's headshot atop, and her heels clicked as she brushed Hana out of the room.

'I'm sorry. We weren't expecting you so soon.'

She had a hoarse voice, but Hana attributed it to her mask. Her cheeks were plastered in heavy makeup, and from her body language, Hana presumed she was a nightmarish producer, where the only creativity she possessed, was drawing her eyebrows every morning.

Darren Joaquim Silva

'I'm Hana, thank you for…'

'Relay your gratitude to the lousy actress who withdrew at short notice.'

She held Hana's headshot to her face and scrutinized her. 'My name is Kira. I am the executive producer. Follow me please.'

She opened a door with a key. It was a large room with a double bed, complete with a dressing table, and vanity mirror.

'This is a lead actors dressing room. If your CV is anything to go by, consider yourself fortunate.'

She walked to a large set of twin doors.

'And this right here… is the stage'

She pushed them open. Hana walked onto the huge stage and marveled at the view. The curtains were velvet red and they matched the sea of cushioned seats. Hana twirled in awe. Her heart pounded her chest. This was everything she'd ever dreamed of.

'So do you accept the role?' asked Kira.

Hana sheepishly brushed her hair behind her ear.

'I still don't know what it is.'

'Metamorphosis by Kafka,' said Satoru, as he hovered across the stage like an ethereal mist.

'Except this is a solo rendition,' he added.

Hana's throat swelled. Performing Kafka was no easy feat. In drama school, his works were tough compulsory reading.

'If you want to accelerate your career from dwindling to sublime, this is the perfect opportunity. So… do you accept the role?' enquired Kira.

Hana blinked hard.

'…Yes.'

◆

"I cannot make you understand. I cannot make anyone understand what is happening inside me."

Hana's voice tinged with a raspy cadence. She hadn't eaten properly in days, and her body was sore from juggling waitressing and the arduous rehearsals.

"…. I cannot make anyone understand what is happening inside me."

Satoru scrunched his face like he'd bit into a sour fruit. 'You have a visceral talent Hana…'

Kira flashed a bewildered glance at him.

'But the opening lines of this play are sacrosanct! In my opinion, no metamorphosis has taken place!'

Hana awkwardly watched as Kira whispered into Satoru's ear. The abrupt scrape of his chair made the company twitch.

'That will be all. Recommence after lunch.'

He popped a cigarette in his mouth and stormed out. Hana dropped her shoulders in fatigue and trudged back to her dressing room. Goose pimples formed on her arms, as a large ventilation shaft blasted the room with chilly wisps of air. There was a loud knock on the door. Kira let herself in. She raised her eyebrows at the tablets scattered across Hana's desk.

'Do you want to quit?' she asked.

Hana rubbed her tired eyes.

'What? No, of course not!'

Kira leaned on the wall beside her.

'I used to be an actress… So I know what you're going through. I shouldn't be telling you this, but if you haven't figured out by now, Satoru directed this very same play here, many years ago.'

'The play that burnt down the theatre?'

'Yes. Apparently he did the same thing to the lead actress then. She was a prodigious talent but he pushed her beyond exhaustion. Some say a "Satoru Nobu production" is often a no win situation.'

Kira shuddered and buttoned her blazer.

'Opening night is in five days. I understand this is a tough role, but if you succeed, you'll make all the headlines. You do want that… don't you?'

'More than anything,' said Hana.

'Good. Now get some rest before we reconvene.'

◆

Hana pirouetted across the stage in agony. Her feet were inflamed, and the floor felt like shards of glass slicing her skin. Satoru threw his hat on the floor.

'Restrict your movement! When in costume, you won't move with such grace!' he yelled.

Hana stared out towards the audience. Her vision blurred and she shook her head. In the back row she spotted her mother and father - watching with great disdain. Her breathing became erratic and she pressed her weight on her back leg. Satoru stood with a worried glance. The trap door of the stage was open and she fell through. Hana screeched and flailed her arms. Suddenly her consciousness swarmed back.

She opened her eyes and realized she was still standing on stage. Satoru leered in disbelief.

'What in the world are you doing?'

'Sorry, I thought I saw someone…'

Hana gasped and forced her eyes open. Her head felt like a heavy weight as she lifted it off the pillow. There was a loud thump on the door.

'You're late again! Get to wardrobe now!'

Hana scrambled out of bed. The batteries in the alarm clock were gone. She scratched her head in confusion and immediately dressed herself. A large man stared at his watch in dismay as Hana burst into the room. He raised her arms and slid a costume over her slender body. He zipped her up and spun her around. When she glanced in the mirror, she stumbled in shock. She looked like a giant fly. It was a hideous outfit; complete with wings, sharp pincers, and a curved abdomen. He ushered her into the basement. A bed was hoisted on chains beside a large dusty mirror. A cobwebbed poster fell from the wall and she grasped it.

"METAMORPHOSIS"

"KITSUNE THEATRE PRODUCTIONS 1978"

In the centre of the picture was a young woman with long hair standing on a stage. All of a sudden the chains rattled as the bed lifted. Hana quickly leapt onto it. A circular light blinded her as the bed ascended.

'Why didn't you say the line?!' queried Satoru.

Hana blinked in uncertainty.

'Your reactions were sublime! But when the bed stops, you pause and deliver the opening line.'

Still disorientated, she nodded in approval.

'From the top!' yelled Satoru.

The piercing whine of a fly awoke her. Hana screamed when she saw herself in the mirror. She hurled her perfume bottle towards the creature in the reflection. The mirror cracked in several pieces. Realizing she was still in costume, she gazed at the fragmented shards in regret.

'What's happening to me?' she muttered.

A fly buzzed and flew into the ventilation shaft as she inspected the label on her sleeping pills.

"NATURAL SLEEP AID. NO SIDE EFFECTS"

◆

There was just enough wind to make the posters around the theatre flutter. Hana stood despondently in the afternoon rain, staring at the snowy peak of Mount Fuji. Her skin was deadly pale and her cheekbones protruded through her malnourished face.

'Satoru is looking for you. What are you doing out here?' inquired Kira.

Hana lethargically turned around. Kira struggled to open her umbrella and her face contorted as her hair became wet.

'Something strange is happening to me Kira… there's something odd about this theatre.'

Kira rolled her eyes. "By believing passionately in something that does not exist, we create it."

'What do you mean?' asked Hana.

'Those are Kafka's words, not mine.'

'No! This is real. You must believe me!'

'You can always quit. Your name isn't on the poster for good reason.'

Hana grit her teeth.

'No! My parents are attending. I have to prove them wrong.'

Her knees gave in and she started to cry.

Kira reluctantly handed her a tissue.

'Nothing I do seems to please Satoru… I haven't eaten or slept in days… and when I'm awake, it feels like I'm hallucinating.'

Kira's phone rang and she answered it.

'Hi Satoru… yes she's outside with me… she needed some fresh air. She'll be along shortly.'

Kira hung up and scowled.

'We open tomorrow! Stop imagining things and get on with it,' she muttered as she dashed inside.

Hana sighed and lethargically admired the wind as it swept a poster off the building.

Opening night finally arrived. Spotlights illuminated the theatre and an elongated red carpet led toward the stage doors. News had spread that the local mayor was attending, and Satoru had invited a plethora of celebrities and critics. Hana spent the entire morning voraciously rehearsing, but the opening lines of the play still tormented her. As she composed herself in the reflection of the cracked mirror, a gut-wrenching stench pervaded the dressing room. Hana anxiously peered at the ventilation shaft. She clambered onto the dressing table and removed the mesh panel. A cluster of flies escaped and whizzed around the room. Her eyebrows contorted. She used her phone as a torch, and crawled into the vent. Hana struggled to hold her breath as the decaying smell penetrated her costume's visor. The buzzing of flies became more audible and her hand pressed into something cold and squishy. She shone her light over. It was a dead fox. Hana screamed and smacked her head against the metal. Her teeth sliced into her tongue and blood swirled around her mouth. Flies were feasting on its flesh and her fingers had broken through its rotting abdomen. She clenched to refrain from vomiting and accidentally fell through a mesh panel. She crashed into a dressing room and coughed sporadically. A laptop was perched on a table, and numerous pills were scattered around it. Her eyes widened as she read the medicinal packaging.

"SIDE EFFECTS MAY INCLUDE DECREASED AWRENESS AND ACUTE HALLUCINATIONS."

The wallpaper on the laptop was a lone woman standing on stage. It was the exact replica of the Kafka poster she'd found in the basement. A facemask and numerous black wigs were hung on the wall. A pang of anger entrenched her body as she stormed out.

Hana pushed the stage doors, but they were locked shut. The entire company was on the red carpet and she spotted her parents in the crowd. Before anyone caught her, she dashed downstairs to the basement. She climbed up the wooden beams and forced open the trapdoor. The auditorium was empty, except for a lone woman standing under the limelight's narrow beam. Hana crept onto the stage and Kira turned to face her. The lights from above revealed an immoral glare of envy that Hana had never before witnessed. A strong odour of gasoline radiated from the velvet curtains beside them.

'It was you... You did this to me?'

Kira replicated her pose on the poster and enunciated to a non-existent audience.

"Confessions and lies are the same. To tell the truth, one must tell lies!"

'What are you talking about?'

'That is also Kafka! But you didn't know that, did you?! Why couldn't you have been like the other actresses and just quit?'

Kira brandished a box of matches.

'No one will ever live to see another actress but me grace this production.'

Hana cautiously stepped backwards.

'I was the lead for this play back in 1978, but moments before the big finale, one of the stage lights fell and struck me.'

Kira removed her facemask and wig. Her scalp was scaled and blistered, and her mouth was severely disfigured.

'Look how much I suffered for my art! And my reward was being recast!' screamed Kira as she struck a match. 'I'll burn you all again! And this time Satoru won't survive!'

Hana knocked aside the matchstick. Kira screamed like a possessed woman and tore a pincer from Hana's costume. She violently slashed Hana's shoulder. Blood poured down Hana's arm and she clutched it in agony. Kira lit another match, but Hana quickly barged her towards the trapdoor. Kira lost her footing and shrieked as she fell down the hole. Hana immediately closed the trapdoor. She unlocked the theatre and frantically ran downstairs. A pool of blood covered the basement and Kira wheezed in pain beside the large cracked mirror. Noise from above rumbled as the guests took their seats. Kira repeatedly tried to grasp the box of matches, but her mangled body wouldn't yield. Hana kicked them aside. Kira's face evolved into a bitter rage. She seized Hana by the throat and mercilessly choked her.

'Let go of me! I need to do this play!'

Hana viciously stabbed her with the pincer. Kira coughed a spew of blood before crashing down dead. Hana stepped back and stared at her hideous insectoid reflection in the mirror.

'No… No! What have I done?'

Tears cascaded down her face as she fell back onto the bed. Suddenly the chains rattled as it ascended. Her heart rapidly thumped as the limelight blinded her.

'… I cannot make you understand! I cannot make anyone understand what is happening inside me! I cannot even explain it to myself!'

The Japan Times: Theatre Guide

"METAMORPHOSIS"

BY

KAFKA

"Hana Izumi shines in a flawless stage debut"

Kafka's wretched tale has been given a chilling update by award winning director Satoru Nobu. This fresh interpretation is the chrysalis the Kitsune Theatre needed to quell its murky history. Although the grotesque costume gives the story a poignant plausibility, Hana Izumi's transformation, from woman to insect is achieved not by tech or fancy lighting, but by sheer acting force. Her visceral delivery of the play's opening line, will haunt many theatregoers for years to come…

KITSUNE THEATRE

Acknowledgements

A medley of writers inspired me to write the second installment of Strange Tales. I highly encourage you to read their works, as I truly am standing on the shoulders of giants. In no particular order I would like to thank…

Aesop
Ray Bradbury
Haruki Murakami
Flannery O Connor
O Henry
Satoshi Kon
Frank R. Stockton
Langston Hughes
Shirley Jackson
Richard Matheson
W.W. Jacobs
Ursula K. Le Guin
Robert F. Young

And last but not least, the heavyweight champion of short stories, and the master of the sting in the tail Roald Dahl.

I would also like to thank my friends; Victor, Gilbert, and Nilan for their critique and appraisal of my work.

Beyond The Luna

The stars no longer twinkle and the moon is broken.
Embark on a danger filled quest and help Luis solve the
mystery that lies **Beyond The Luna.**

Echo In The Forest

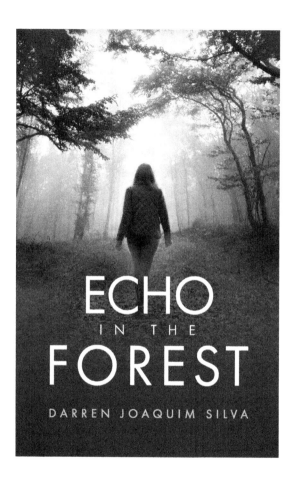

Struggling to find her missing parents, Echo ventures into the very place they warned her about, the forest. But an unspoken darkness looms under the trees, delighting in her sorrow and biding its time in… **Echo In The Forest.**

Strange Tales

Inspired by Roald Dahl's short classics. These nine tales of intrigue and deception all contain a twist, so read **Strange Tales** with a watchful eye.

Social Media

I always love hearing from you, please follow me on…

Twitter **@djoaquimsilva**

#StrangeTales2

Synopsis

Don't Dance With Tomorrow – Encountering a fortune-teller, a woman becomes obsessed with foresight. But pays an enormous price for interfering with fate.

The Prince – A travelling prince engages in a series of barbaric challenges for his right to marry the princess.

One Fine Day – Stranded in the rural countryside, a married couple are offered help from a peculiar family.

Ace In The Hole – After a bitter exchange with a rival, a mad scientist deems defamation intellectually unsatisfying, and plots the ultimate revenge.

The Lights Are On But Nobody's Home – A single mother spends the night in a derelict apartment, but the previous guests haven't entirely checked out.

Only God Forgives – Narrowly escaping a heinous assault, an elderly woman peculiarly invites the perpetrator over for dinner.

Yesterday Was Beautiful - Self-isolating due to a deadly virus; a bitter war veteran encounters a strange girl who rekindles his love for life.

The Falcon & The Viper – Crowning himself king of the jungle, a villainous snake challenges the animals to a foul game of survival of the fittest.

Encore – A down on her luck actress accepts a mysterious stage role. But the theatres horrific past distorts her sense of reality.

Darren Joaquim Silva

Notes

Darren Joaquim Silva

Printed in Great Britain
by Amazon